TORAN'S ENCHANTRESS

A HIGHLANDER FATE NOVELLA

STELLA KNIGHT

This novella takes place after the events in the main *Highlander Fate* series, featuring a character who appears in the series as a background character—the matchmaking *stiuireadh*, Kensa. While this novella is a standalone and can be read without having read the other books in the series, please be aware that there are references to events that occurred during the main series.

I hope you love reading Kensa's story as much as I loved writing it. Enjoy!

PRONUNCIATION GUIDE

Artair - AHR-tər
Toran - TO-rin
Iain - EE-ən
Caomhain - KEE-van
Muire - MEE-yur
Eilys - AY-lis
Gormelia - GORM-eel-yuh
Ceitidh - KAY-tee
Fiadha - FEE-uh

CHAPTER 1

1395
Scottish Highlands

Kensa watched her niece, Diana, and Diana's husband, Artair, playing with their twin boys, a smile curving her lips. She loved seeing her niece so happy. Diana had rarely seemed so content in her own time . . . the twenty-first century.

As if reading her mind, Diana met her gaze and smiled. They were all gathered in Artair and Diana's large private chamber in their manor; it was Diana's ancestral home that Artair had purchased for her. They'd made the sprawling manor into a cozy family home, perfect for their adorable three-year-old twin boys. Kensa wasn't the only frequent visitor to their manor; Artair's sister

Liosa, her husband Keagan, and their daughter Ainslee, who lived nearby, also came by often for visits.

Kensa returned Diana's smile, amusement filling her as she recalled Diana's once staunch refusal to ever use her time-traveling ability. Not only had she used it, she'd fallen in love in the past and chosen to stay with her beloved.

Both Kensa and Diana were *stiuireadh*, witches with the ability to travel through time. Kensa had spent many years as a sort of magical matchmaker, bringing lovers together who were separated by the chasm of time. She'd loved her days of matchmaking, watching couples she'd brought together happily settling into their lives.

She'd recently decided to end her time as a matchmaker, content with the myriad of couples she'd brought together. If she was being honest with herself, Kensa had begun to feel . . . restless in recent years. Every time she visited Diana, a strange longing had pierced her, especially when she noticed the loving looks Diana and Artair shared.

Now fifty-two, Kensa had never made time for love in her own life, content with the platonic relationships she had with the witches in her coven and her familial ties. She'd simply assumed that love was not written in the stars for her; she was the one who joined soul mates together, and she'd been fine with that until that persistent restlessness—a yawning ache of loneliness—had begun to grow within her. An ache that she couldn't seem to rid herself of.

She shook her head as if to clear it of those troubling thoughts. At her age, she needed to accept that love had passed her by. She just needed another project, something else to explore. She'd briefly considered resuming her matchmaking but knew that would only make that ache within her grow. Instead, she'd decided to take on another time-travel task to occupy her: a mystery that both fascinated and perplexed her.

"Come join us," Diana said, pulling Kensa from her thoughts. Diana gestured to the table where a servant had just set up dinner; Artair and the boys were now settling in. Kensa had been so consumed by her thoughts she hadn't even noticed the servant enter.

Kensa obliged, sitting down next to little Artair, named after his father, placing a kiss onto his golden-blond head, love coursing through her. She absolutely adored Diana's boys, and they doted on her as well. Diana had joked that they seemed to enjoy Kensa's presence more than their own parents.

They ate a delicious meal of salted pork, vegetables, and bread as Artair and Diana told Kensa about several travelers they'd assisted during the past few weeks. After deciding to stay in this time, Diana had used her magical abilities to assist wayward travelers who found themselves in the past. Kensa was proud of her niece for undertaking such a task. For someone who had once denounced magic and turned her back on it, she now fully embraced it.

As Kensa listened to her niece describe assisting a traveler from the Victorian era, who had landed in this time by accident, her thoughts kept returning to her own upcoming journey to the past. Her preoccupation must have been obvious, because after the boys' nurse came to fetch them for bed and led them from the chamber, Diana turned to face Kensa with a concerned frown.

"Aunt Kensa, what's wrong?"

Kensa hesitated. She'd held off on telling Diana what her plans were; she knew her niece would just worry about her. But she figured it was best to get it out of the way.

"Now that I'm done with my matchmaking, there's a mystery I've been wanting to solve. The mystery of Tairseach."

Both Diana and Artair's eyes widened. They, along with many others who dwelled in the Highlands, were well aware of the mysterious village of Tairseach. Tairseach was the portal through which travelers made their way through time, an ancient village that now lay in ruins.

No one knew much about Tairseach, other than it had once been a dwelling of the druids, ancestors of the stiuireadh, until they'd mysteriously disappeared and the village had fallen into ruin. If any other traveler or stiuireadh had solved— or attempted to solve—the mystery of what had happened before, they'd never revealed it. To this day, even the most seasoned stiuireadh didn't know what had truly happened in the ancient village.

"I'd like to go back in time to determine what really happened there," she continued.

As expected, her niece stiffened, worry flickering across her expression. "I don't know if it's safe for you to—"

"I'll be fine. You know I'll take care," she assured her, but Diana didn't look convinced.

"Will you go alone?" Diana asked. Her gaze flickered to Artair before returning to Kensa. "Maybe I should come with—"

"That's not necessary, sweetheart. You stay with your family."

"But Kensa—"

"I ken of another who wants tae ken what happened in Tairseach," Artair interrupted. "He's called Toran; he's a clan noble. We spoke at the last feast and Tairseach came up. He's one of the few in the Highlands who kens of time travel; he has ancestors who were stiuireadh. Several of his ancestors once lived in Tairseach and vanished; he told me he's always wanted tae ken what truly happened. He's an honorable man. Perhaps he can join ye."

Diana looked encouraged by this, but Kensa was wary. When not accompanying someone to the past, she'd traveled on her own and preferred it that way. She'd looked forward to taking this adventure on her own.

"I think you should talk to this man," Diana said, giving her a pleading look. "I'd feel better about this if there was someone with you. And you know the past—I hate it too, but women are always safer with a male companion."

Kensa heaved a sigh, meeting Diana's pleading eyes. Though still wary, she loved her niece and could deprive her of nothing.

"Very well," she said. "I'll at least meet with this man."

IT WAS the very next day when she was introduced to Toran. She'd just returned from a walk through the nearby forest with the boys when she emerged to find Artair approaching her, trailed by a tall, broad-shouldered man.

He had dark, wavy hair shot through with strands of silver-gray eyes, and strong, aristocratic features. His white tunic and blue belted plaid kilt highlighted his muscular frame well.

Kensa halted in her tracks, her breath hitching. He was the most handsome man she had ever seen. A sudden, dizzying sense of déjà vu struck her. But Kensa was certain she'd never seen this man before; she definitely would have remembered him.

"Kensa," Artair said, gesturing to the man with a smile. "This is Toran. He'll be yer companion tae the past."

CHAPTER 2

oran took in the lovely lass before him, struck by her beauty. Artair had told him the woman was Diana's older aunt, but she didn't look much older than her niece. Her hair was even darker than his, black as a raven's wings, and her hazel eyes seemed to shift in color as she gazed up at him. With her feminine features and delectable curves that he could detect even beneath her loose-fitting cloak, she was much bonnier than he'd anticipated.

"Lady Kensa," he said, trying to keep his voice neutral as he gave her a formal nod.

"Y—you can just call me Kensa," Kensa stammered, her soft voice as lovely as her features.

"I'll leave ye tae discuss," Artair said, giving them both a long, lingering look before swinging his two giggling sons up into his arms and heading back to the manor.

Kensa watched Artair go, looking as if she

wanted to ask him to stay, and Toran felt a stab of guilt. He knew she was from a time yet to come; perhaps men from that time did not act with honor.

"Kensa," he said, and those lovely eyes turned to focus back on him. "Ye have no need tae be fearful of me. I am a man of honor, something my sons and Artair will attest tae."

She looked taken aback for a moment. "I'm sure you are," she said, with a polite smile. "Shall we discuss inside? It's chilly out."

She tugged her cloak closer to her body, and Toran had the sudden, strong desire to pull her close, to warm her with his body, a thought he quickly forced away. He'd just met the lass, assured her he was honorable, and he was already having inappropriate thoughts about her.

He trailed Kensa back into the manor, keeping a respectable distance, but he couldn't stop himself from admiring the curve of her hips or the way they swayed when she walked.

She led him into a spacious drawing room where a fire roared in the fireplace. She discarded her cloak, placing it on a chair, and warmed her hands over the fire, revealing a gown of deep scarlet that put her generous bosom on display. He made himself avert his eyes.

"Artair mentioned you have ancestors who were stiuireadh?" she asked.

"Aye," he said. "My great-grandmother. I donnae have magic myself, nor did my parents, but 'tis possible for me tae travel through time as the stiuireadh do."

He could recall his great-grandmother, still alive when he was a wee lad, sitting him on her lap and telling him she saw travels through time in his future. She was the one who'd told him tales of his druid ancestors who'd vanished long ago in Tairseach. He'd always wanted to know what had truly happened there; he'd even sought out stiuireadh over the years to see if they could uncover the mystery for him, but they had no more answers than he did.

When Artair told him his wife's aunt was traveling back in time to solve the mystery, excitement had surged through him at both the chance to travel for the first time and to find out what had happened in Tairseach all those years ago.

"Have you ever traveled through time?" she asked.

"No. My life has always been here in the present. I wanted tae be here for my family—my wife and sons."

A shadow crossed her face. "Your wife knows of your interest and your intent to travel now?"

"My wife died many years ago," he said. "And my sons are grown with families of their own."

"I'm sorry." Kensa gave him a sympathetic smile. "About your wife."

He merely offered her a polite nod. He'd cared for his late wife, Lyssa, and treasured the time they'd had together. When she'd died of plague over ten years ago, he'd grieved her, but that grief was but a shadow now.

"Time travel is a wondrous—but dangerous—thing," Kensa continued, studying him closely. "If you escort me to the past, you need to listen to my guidance every step of the way. Are you certain this is what you want to do?"

"Aye," he said, without hesitation. Even sitting on his great-grandmother's knee long ago, he'd wondered what it would be like to travel through time, but his duties to his clan and to his family had kept him firmly in the present. "And ye?"

She looked offended. "What do you mean?"

"I've no wife; my children are grown men," he said. An odd feeling churned in his belly as he pressed, "Yer husband has no objection tae yer traveling through time with a man ye donnae ken? Yer children?"

She stiffened, averting her gaze. "I've no children and no husband. My life has been dedicated to magic and time travel. I only agreed to travel with someone because my niece worries for me."

He didn't understand the relief that coursed through him when she told him she had no husband. *It doesnae matter if she has no husband,* he scolded himself. But the relief remained.

"Verrae well," he said. "Tell me what I need tae ken before we leave."

〜

"Is she bonnie?" his son, Iain, asked. "The stiuireadh ye're traveling with?"

Toran gave his eldest son a playful scowl. He'd invited his two adult sons over to dinner at his manor to tell them of his plans, bracing himself for their protests. Instead, they both seemed more curious about his traveling companion.

Aye, she's bonnie, he thought. *Possibly the bonniest lass I've ever laid eyes upon. Distractingly so.*

"That doesnae matter, son," he said gruffly. "I'm nae traveling for any other reason than tae uncover what happened tae our druid ancestors."

His younger son, Caomhain, reached out to grip his shoulder. "We jest with ye. We just want tae see ye content."

"I am content," he said firmly.

His parents had arranged his marriage to his late wife Lyssa; she was the daughter of a fellow clan noble. Their match had not been one of great passion, but he'd cared deeply for her and she for him. He'd not had the desire to remarry since Lyssa's passing; he was in his fifty-fifth year and had his two heirs, he was happy with his life as it was. Though he enjoyed the occasional mistress, he had dedicated his life to tending to his manor and his lands, serving his clan, and being there for his sons.

"Are ye nae afeared?" Iain asked. "Of traveling through time?"

"No," Toran said. He found the prospect

daunting, but his excitement was greater than any misgiving he could have.

"Ye're braver than I, Father," Iain said.

"'Tis nae difficult," Caomhain teased his brother. "Ye've been a coward since ye were a lad."

Iain gave Caomhain a mock scowl before turning to his father. "Will ye take care when ye travel?" he asked. "I want ye tae be around tae see yer grandson born."

Though Iain's expression and tone were light, Toran could sense the portent there. Iain had been close to his mother and her death had wieghed heavily upon him; he knew his son was genuinely worried for him. He leaned forward, holding Iain's gaze. "Ye ken I will—for ye, Caomhain and my grandchildren."

At Toran's assurance, Iain's shoulders relaxed. Caomhain then inquired after Iain's wife, and his two sons began to swap tales of fatherhood. Both of his sons were wed to good lasses they loved; Caomhain had a wee daughter while Iain had a young son and another on the way. Pride coursed through him as he studied his sons; he knew Lyssa would also have been proud of the men they had become.

A sudden, unbidden thought of Kensa came into his mind, and he wondered if she would like his sons, and they her. But he dismissed the thought; Kensa was his guide and companion to the past, nothing more. There would be no cause for her to ever meet his sons.

It soon grew late, and his sons gave him long embraces, urging him again to take care and promising to tend to his manor and his lands while he was gone. As they rode off into the night to their own homes, he pondered the words Caomhain had posed to him earlier that evening. *We just want tae see ye content.*

Again, an unbidden image of Kensa's lovely features flickered through his mind, but he dismissed it. *I'm content with my life as it is*, he told himself. *I am.*

Yet the bonnie witch lingered in his thoughts for the remainder of the evening and into the night, following him into his dreams.

CHAPTER 3

Kensa spent the day before they were to depart preparing for their time in the past.

On her own, she'd reviewed the records kept on Tairseach in one of her coven's grimoires. Other stiuireadh who'd tried to solve the mystery of Tairseach had done so in what they believed was the simplest way, by traveling to the time it was thought to have fallen into ruin—the year 915. Yet no witch had been able to get close to that year, leading many stiuireadh to believe that time itself didn't want the mystery to be solved.

Kensa had learned during her years as a stiuireadh that some events in the past and the future were set in stone and could not be changed; many witches believed that the mysterious abandonment of Tairseach was one of them. If that were the case, Kensa could accept it. If not, she was determined to uncover the mystery of Tairseach's fate.

She was going to attempt a complicated Time Weaving spell to get as close as possible to the time Tairseach had fallen into ruin, closer than any stiuireadh had gotten before. If she couldn't do that, then her journey would be over before it had even started.

She explained all this to Toran over a map of the Highlands that Artair had given her when he came to the manor that evening.

"Yer niece has told me ye're a powerful stiuireadh," he said in response. "If anyone can get us tae the right time, I believe 'tis ye."

His gray eyes held hers for a disconcertingly long moment. Kensa swallowed and looked away, moved by the unwavering faith he already had in her.

"If we are able to get close enough to 915, I plan to go to the coven that was nearest to Tairseach at the time using a Locator spell; they should be able to inform us of what happened. I'm hoping that the stiuireadh who fled from Tairseach are in this coven," Kensa continued. With Diana's help, Kensa had learned that the coven nearest to Tairseach was located on the outskirts of a small village called Aillin.

"And when we get tae this time?" Toran asked.

"There are cottages the stiuireadh have access to in various time periods they travel to—they serve as way stations of sorts. For the time we're going to, there's a small cottage near Aillin where we can stay," Kensa said, pointing to a location on the map. "We use Cloaking spells to shield such cottages from view when a stiuireadh isn't using it."

He nodded, a look of awe infusing his expression. After a moment, he leaned forward, training those intense gray eyes of his on her.

"What is it like?" he asked. "Traveling through time?"

"It's difficult to describe," she said, after a brief pause. "It's like . . . falling. From a great height. And the sensation of a substantial amount of time passing, only you're standing still. It's exhilarating, really."

He frowned, looking confused. "Exhilarating?"

Kensa gave him an apologetic look; she was usually better at choosing her words when interacting with someone from a different time. Exhilaration was a word that wouldn't come into use for centuries from this time. "Happiness," she corrected. "A joy so complete it almost takes your breath away. At least that's how I feel when I travel through time."

"Ah," he said, his lips curving into a smile. "Then I look forward tae the journey."

He kept his gaze on her, and Kensa fought the urge to look away, even as she felt a flush rise to her cheeks.

What on earth is wrong with me? Kensa wondered. She was over fifty years old, not some blushing virgin. It wasn't as if she'd never been around attractive men before. Many of her travelers were handsome men, but she'd not felt the slightest inkling of attraction toward them.

But there was something different about Toran. The other men she'd helped guide through time had simply not been for her. Toran seemed as if . . . he fit. With her.

That's ridiculous, she chided herself. She was his guide to the past, and he was her escort. That was the extent of their relationship.

She stood abruptly, breaking the silent spell between them. "Well, I suppose you'll need to get some rest," she said. "I'll see you just after first light tomorrow."

Was she mistaken, or was there a flash of disappointment in his eyes? If there was, it quickly vanished as he got to his feet and gave her a hasty nod.

"On the morrow," he echoed, giving her one last look before exiting the drawing room.

AT JUST PAST dawn the next morning, Kensa embraced Diana, Artair, and their two sons goodbye in the manor's entryway, promising she would be careful, before joining Toran outside.

Her heart rate accelerated at the sight of him; he looked sinfully handsome in a belted plaid kilt of forest green with a white tunic. Desire darted through her, which she made herself ignore. She needed to focus on the journey ahead, not her sexy traveling companion.

After waving goodbye one last time to Diana and Artair, she and Toran left the manor grounds, heading toward the small patch of forest where Kensa could use her magic to transport them both without any servants witnessing their departure. Kensa could travel to the past from anywhere, but given that Tairseach was her focus, she wanted to travel to the past directly from within its ruins, hoping to draw on its magic to pull her back to the right time.

She came to a stop in the first small clearing they arrived at. She reached out to take Toran's hand, trying to not react to the searing heat that spread throughout her body when her fingers met his.

Toran met her gaze, nothing but trust in his eyes, and it again struck her how much faith he was putting in her to see him safely to the past. Even though he was ostensibly coming as her male escort, a sudden protectiveness surged through her. She would keep him safe, no matter what they faced in the past.

Taking a deep breath and forcing herself to concentrate, Kensa murmured the words of the spell that would transport them to Tairseach.

"Gabh sinn gu Tairseach . . ."

The sensation of a swirling vortex of wind tugged on their bodies, and the world dissolved around them. When it came into focus again, they stood in the center of Tairseach.

Kensa released Toran's hand and took it in. Around them, Tairseach lay in ruin—old cottages and buildings which nature had slowly reclaimed. On its edge sat an old castle that was a mere shadow of the fortress it must have been. She'd gotten used to seeing Tairseach as a ruined place, a place of mystery and long-dead magic. And now she would—hopefully—discover what had truly happened here.

At her side, Toran took in the ruins of the village with a quiet look of awe. "I've only been here once before. It feels . . . it feels . . . " He trailed off, searching for the right words.

"Like it's calling out to you somehow," Kensa finished for him.

Toran gave her a nod of agreement. "Aye," he said.

They shared a quiet moment of reverence as Kensa surveyed their surroundings. How many times had she come here, guiding travelers through time to find their soul mates? And now, she was about to take her own adventure.

Toran trailed her to the ruins of the castle, where she turned to face him.

"Are you ready?" she asked. "It's not too late to go back to the manor. Time travel can be—"

"Ye've prepared me well. I'm ready," Toran interrupted, his tone filled with resolve.

Kensa nodded, reaching out to take his hand.

Again, that rush of awareness swept over her, along with a sense of . . . togetherness. A unity she'd never felt with any other traveler she'd guided to the past. Feeling a sense of calm, she murmured the words of the spell that would cast them back through time.

"*Snàithlean ùine, cluinn mo ghairm. Snàithlean ùine, cluinn mo tagradh. Treòraich mi gu sàbhailte tron t-slighe agad chun àm a dh'fhalbh . . .*"

CHAPTER 4

Unknown Time
Unknown Place

They arrived on the edge of a sprawling glen.

Toran stumbled to his knees, gasping for air. Kensa had been right. He felt as if he'd just fallen from a great height.

After Kensa murmured the words of the spell, the world had dissolved around them. There was blackness, a blackness through which he felt himself hurtling. A multitude of sensations had pulled at him, but the most prominent was the sensation of the vastness of time itself swirling around him: births, deaths, and everything in between.

He still felt out of sorts and looked up at Kensa

as he struggled to catch his breath. She stood several yards away from him, looking both serene and lovely as she studied him with concern. Embarrassment filled him at his disorientation; he tried to appear unaffected as he pulled himself to his full height, but he stumbled once more. Kensa hurried forward, helping him straighten.

"How do you feel?" she asked gently.

"'I'm—well," he lied, giving her an abrupt nod.

Kensa's lovely lips twitched with amusement. "It's okay to admit that you're shaken," she said. "Many travelers I guide through time have to take a moment to steady themselves. The first time I traveled I lost my last meal."

This made him feel better, until he realized that she must have been a wee lass when she first traveled through time.

"I'm well," he repeated, but he allowed his lips to relax in a smile. She returned it, her smile as radiant as the rays of the midday sun, and for a moment he forgot all about his discomfort.

She turned away from him, gazing at something in the distance. He followed her gaze, seeing nothing but nature in their immediate surroundings. Where was the cottage? And how would they know if they were in the right place? The right time?

"*Nochdaidh mi am bothan dhomh,*" Kensa murmured, and a thatched-roof cottage appeared in the distance.

Toran stared at the cottage, agape. Kensa had

told him of the magically cloaked cottage, and he'd just traveled through time, but it was still awe-inspiring to see her magic at work. Not only was she desirable, she wielded great power with ease.

Kensa was already moving toward it, and Toran trailed her, taking in their surroundings. From the wilderness around them; the vast glen, the patches of forest in the near distance, the expanse of a cloudless blue sky above, it could have been any time.

Yet something in his bones told him they were far from the time he was born in.

They arrived at the cottage, which was sparse, comprising only one room with a dusty stone floor, a hearth in the center, and several bed pallets stacked in the corner next to a small chest.

"I'm sorry it's so sparse," Kensa said, moving over to the hearth and murmuring a spell to light it. "I know you're used to the finery of manors and castles."

He stiffened. He knew she didn't mean it as an affront. Aye, he was a wealthy man, but he was capable of dwelling in a simple cottage for a short time. He'd slept in worse circumstances whenever his clan went into battle and he'd had to sleep on the ground with the other men.

"This cottage will serve well," he said.

Kensa moved over to the chest and opened it, pulling out a simple, worn men's tunic, one that looked even more worn than one his servants would wear. Her gaze slid to the fine clothing he wore and she gave him an apologetic look.

He strode toward her before she could speak. "I may be a wealthy man," he said, giving her a firm look, "but I'm nae so coddled I'll refuse tae wear an old tunic."

"That's—not what I was going to say," Kensa fumbled. "I was going to say—" She flushed, dipping her eyes, and continued, "that you may be too—broad—for this tunic."

Her eyes roamed over his muscular chest, her cheeks turning rosy. His annoyance dissipated as pleasure filled him at her words, and he studied the tunic closely. It would be a slim fit, but it would fit.

"It will fit, lass," he said, giving her a gentle smile.

Kensa averted her gaze, still looking disconcerted. "Ah—there are stores of dried food here, barley and oats, that we can eat for now. There's also a small amount of water in this jar for us to use until we can find a freshwater source. We can purchase other food we need from the market in Ailin; there's coin here as well. We can seek out the coven tomorrow. In the meantime, I'm going to perform some Seeking spells; I want to confirm exactly where and when we are."

Amazement filled him that she could determine such things using her magic. He wondered if he'd ever get used to what this lovely witch was capable of.

"I can prepare something for us tae eat while ye work yer spells," he said.

Kensa's eyes widened with surprise, and he chuckled. "Aye, there are cooks in my manor, but there were times I had tae prepare my own food when I traveled with the clan. And I prepared meals for my sons when they were lads."

"I need to stop underestimating you," Kensa said, giving him a wan smile.

"Aye," he agreed. "Ye go tend tae yer spells. I'll prepare our meal."

Still smiling, Kensa exited the cottage, and he moved to one of the open windows, watching as she walked away, unable to tear his gaze away from the seductive sway of her hips.

When she disappeared into the patch of forest nearby, he took in the surroundings, another sliver of awe passing through him at the realization that he was in another time, along with a stab of regret. Perhaps he should have used his ability to travel through time sooner; it had been a long while since his sons had needed him.

He shook off the feeling of regret. Even though he'd just met Kensa, he was glad that the person he'd traveled back in time with was with her. Traveling through time with her at his side felt right. *Just as my guide*, he told himself firmly. He would have to take care to mitigate his desire for her.

Using the small jar of water stashed next to the dry food stores, he prepared a simple porridge made of oats and barley. The barley was simmering over the hearth in a pot when Kensa returned, a look of relief on her face.

"I saw a village in the near distance through the forest. My Seeking spell confirmed that it's Ailin. As for the time, I could determine we're in the right century, the tenth. But we'll have to confirm the exact year from the coven."

Relief filled him as well, and as they sat down before the hearth to eat, he studied her with curiosity. "How were ye able tae determine the year with yer magic?"

"It's a combination spell—a Seeking and a Summoning. I summon images from the century we're in as well as seek events I know happened in this century," Kensa said calmly.

It would indeed take him time to get used to what she could do, something she seemed to take for granted. He had to remind himself that magic for her must be as normal as breathing.

"Ye said ye've traveled often," he said, wanting to know more about her abilities. "How many times?"

"I've lost count," she said. "I traveled for the first time when I was a girl. My mother was the leader of our coven; both she and my father were powerful stiuireadh. They taught me all the ins and outs of time travel, including the history and culture of each time I traveled to. Some stiuireadh travel out of necessity—to right wrongs that time allows to be fixed in the past, or out of curiosity about what different times are really like. I chose to

be a matchmaker, to bring together couples separated by time. There's nothing like the joy I felt
uniting those couples. I did that for many years,
and I enjoyed it, until . . ."

She trailed off, an unreadable expression flickering across her face before she continued, "Until I
decided it was time for a change."

He watched her closely, suspecting that she
was hiding the true reason she'd stopped matchmaking. Yet he instinctively knew that questioning
her further would only make her more reticent.

"I cannae believe this is possible," he said,
deciding to switch topics. "That I am here in the
past, as I've long been wont tae do. I thank ye,
Kensa, for taking me with ye."

She met his gaze . . . and he felt it. An intan-
gible pull of desire. Kensa flushed and lowered her
gaze, shifting the subject to what they would do the
next day, but that heat—that pull—lingered.

He wondered how long he would be able to
resist its pull.

Just after dawn the next morning, Toran
walked alongside Kensa as they headed to Ailin,
which Kensa had pointed out to him was due west,
through the patch of forest. He tried not to focus on
how lovely she looked in her simple, green over-
dress and cloak, which intensified the hazel of her
eyes.

The night before, they'd retired to separate bed pallets on opposite sides of the cottage to sleep. He'd respectfully left the cottage when she changed into her underdress for the night, trying not to think of the naked curves of her body.

It took him a good long while to get to sleep.

"Here we are," Kensa murmured at his side, pulling him back to the present, and he followed her gaze.

At the sight of the village ahead, even without Kensa's confirmation, he could tell they were in another time. It was much smaller than the villages of his time, consisting of simple thatched-roof cottages, farmsteads, and miniscule woven-wood and daub buildings. The people milling to-and-fro were wearing simpler tunics than the people of his time. The finery of his fourteenth-century attire would have certainly stood out.

Kensa kept her head low as if trying to look inconspicuous, and he did the same as they skirted the village. It seemed to work; other than a few curious stares, few seemed to pay them any mind.

Kensa seemed to know where to go, making her way to the far edge of the village, homing in on several cottages that were clustered together. She paused, glancing up at him.

"Those cottages are where the local coven lives," she said, gesturing toward the cottages up ahead. "Let me do the talking. Stiuireadh of the past aren't very trusting of outsiders."

He nodded his acquiescence, and they made their way to the nearest cottage.

Before they reached it, the door swung open, and a young flame-haired woman stepped out, glaring at Kensa. Kensa opened her mouth to speak, but the woman interrupted her.

"I ken ye're a stiuireadh from a time yet tae come. I've foreseen yer arrival. I ken what ye seek, but 'tis none of yer concern. Go back tae yer own time and donnae return."

CHAPTER 5

Frustration surged through Kensa as she and Toran left the village. Though she knew stiuireadh from the past were wary of outsiders, she'd not even considered that one would refuse to even hear her out. Foolishly, she hadn't planned on any other alternative to finding out what happened at Tairseach.

She slid a glance at Toran, who gave her a sympathetic look. Embarrassment swept over her; she'd brought Toran to this time and she'd already failed in their intended task. Solving historical mysteries wasn't her usual forte; her expertise had been bringing lovers together, and that typically only involved getting the two people who belonged together in the same timeline. After that, it was up to the pull of mutual attraction, love, and fate to do the rest.

Perhaps she'd gone too far in attempting to assuage her loneliness. Having a handsome Highlander such as Toran as her traveling companion had only intensified those feelings; he'd caused a desire to spike in her that she'd never felt before.

She jerked in surprise when Toran's hand took hers, forcing her out of her thoughts and back to the present. Startled, she looked up at him. He gave her a gentle smile, causing her insides to flutter.

"Trust me," he said simply.

Keeping her hand in his, he led her behind him into the patch of forest through which they'd came, but instead of continuing down the path that led to the cottage, he led her to a creek that snaked through a small clearing. Only then did he let go of her hand, the action leaving her feeling oddly bereft, and gestured to the creek.

"I can tell ye're troubled. Whenever I need tae mull over a problem, I like tae go tae the nearest body of water tae think or tae ease my worries. There's something about the sound of rushing water that soothes me. When my sons were lads, they fought often. I would take them tae a nearby creek—which seemed tae calm them—tae settle whatever matter was between them."

Kensa considered his words and surveyed the creek. A sense of calm ebbed her frustration as she took in the peaceful scene, the sunlight glittering off the waters, the rushing sound of water over the rocks.

She closed her eyes and took a deep breath, trying to gather her bearings. Though she still felt lingering frustration, Toran was right . . . there was something about the rushing waters that soothed her. The ancient magic of the druids that flowed through her veins seemed to strengthen whenever nature surrounded her; it was why she preferred to perform her spells outdoors.

"I can talk tae the young stiuireadh," Toran said, after a long pause. "I'll go tae her as someone with no magic, who just wants tae ken what happened tae my ancestors who once dwelled in Tairseach. Perhaps I'll remind her of a father, or a grandfather, and she'll take pity on me and help us."

Kensa's lips twitched with amusement, her gaze raking over his handsome form. "I doubt she'll believe you're a grandfather," she muttered, before she could stop herself.

A look of surprise flared in his eyes, and a gentle smile curved his lips. He stepped forward, and pressed, "I can try tae convince her tae help us."

Kensa bit her lip, mulling over his suggestion. He was right; the young witch may take pity on him, and right now she had no other option but to seek the help of stiuireadh in this time.

"All right. I suppose it's worth a try," she said finally. "But I think we should wait until tomorrow. Hopefully other members of the coven will be there, and even if she still turns us away, perhaps they won't."

They returned to the cottage, where Toran prepared them another meal of porridge, and they sat side by side before the hearth to eat. Though it was a simple meal, it was surprisingly tasty.

"Lyssa taught me how tae make even bland meals appealing for our sons," he said, seeming to read her mind.

He smiled at the memory, and Kensa forced herself to return it, unable to stem a stab of jealousy that she had no right to feel. He'd been married to this Lyssa and fathered two sons with her. It was all but a given that he still harbored feelings for her. Another reminder for Kensa to stem her desire for him.

"I hope I can convince the coven tae help us on the morrow," he continued. "I have some experience with bringing people over tae my side. Whenever there was a conflict between the clan nobles, the chieftain often relied on me tae help bring about peace."

Kensa couldn't help but give him a teasing smile. "Stiuireadh aren't clan nobles. We're far more difficult."

"Aye," he said, returning her smile, "but the process remains the same. I would hear both sides and often realize that both want the same thing, yet they want tae achieve it in different ways."

"So, you were not only the peacemaker between your two sons, but between members of your clan as well?"

"Aye," he said. "I think I can handle stubborn stiuireadh."

"Let's hope so," she said with a sigh, reaching

out to warm her hands before the hearth. Toran did the same, their hands brushing against each other, and though it was a mere millisecond of contact, the searing heat that flared within Kensa was electric.

Their eyes locked, and she suddenly became very aware of Toran's proximity. It seemed as if an invisible force was pulling her toward him as he leaned forward, seizing her lips with his.

Kensa's heart rate skyrocketed as they kissed. She felt herself leaning in close to him as he probed her mouth with his, winding his hands through her hair. They were pressed so close together that their hearts hammered together as one. An aching need coursed through her as he held her tight against his muscular frame, his kiss growing even more demanding, along with a fervent desire for him to never let her go.

CHAPTER 6

Toran didn't think he could ever let her go.

As his lips probed hers, long dormant feelings rose to the surface—desire, passion, an aching need. Her lush curves pressed against his made his arousal swell, and he held her even closer as he devoured her mouth with his own.

When she let out a soft whimper, his arousal spiked even more, and he wound his hands through the silken strands of her hair, delving his tongue into her mouth, wondering if she tasted this sweet between her thighs. The very thought caused a guttural moan to erupt from his mouth as he deepened the kiss with a sudden possessive need to make her lips swollen from his kiss.

When they finally broke apart, breathless, she looked even more lovely: her hazel eyes husky with desire, cheeks flushed, bosom heaving. The silence between them stretched, filled with only the sound of their heavy breaths, until Kensa seemed to come to her senses, stumbling to her feet as if emerging from a trance.

"I—I should work on some of my spells," she stammered, hurrying to the door and leaving before he could stop her.

He watched her to go, an unexpected wave of hurt, then shame, sweeping over him. Since first laying eyes on her, he'd promised himself that he'd act honorably despite his desire for her, and he'd already broken that promise.

But she had returned his kiss—eagerly. Again, a fierce arousal arose within him as he recalled how she'd pressed her body to his, her lovely mouth submitting to the forceful demand of his kiss: the soft little moan she'd made as he'd probed her mouth with his. He'd felt her desire, almost as intense as his own.

Still, she clearly regretted the kiss, as she couldn't wait to get away from him afterward. He told himself he'd apologize, that he wouldn't act dishonorably toward her again, even as regret filled him at the very thought. He was here in this time to uncover the mystery of what had happened to his ancestors at Tairseach, not to seduce the stiuireadh who was his escort to the past.

Before meeting Kensa, he could always control his desire for any lass he found bonnie, yet there was something different about the lovely witch. Something that made him want her more than he'd ever wanted anyone, including Lyssa.

At this realization, he waited for the guilt to come, but there was none. Though he'd cared deeply for his wife, theirs had not been a union of passion. He'd just assumed he'd never have great passion for anyone.

Kensa had changed that.

She didn't return to the cottage until the sky was darkening and he'd begun to worry. As soon as she entered the cottage, he stepped forward, intending to apologize and reiterate his honor, but she seemed to know what he was going to say, holding up her hand and shaking her head.

"It's all right," she said, not looking at him. "I went to the forest to practice Seeking spells that may be useful in this time. I also gathered these mushrooms from the forest. We can add them to the porridge for supper."

Their meal was tense as they shared stilted conversation about what they planned to do the next day; he missed the easy conversation they'd shared earlier. Kensa kept avoiding his eyes, and after they'd eaten, she wished him a good night before retiring to her corner of the cottage. He politely turned away as she stripped down to her underdress and slid into her pallet, ignoring his simmering desire.

Though they were only a few yards apart as they drifted off to sleep on their separate pallets, he couldn't help but feel as if there was an ocean between them.

~

THE NEXT MORNING, Toran and Kensa returned to the cottages where the coven dwelled. As Kensa had predicted, there were now several other stiuireadh, including a petite one holding a baby in her arms, and the young witch who'd turned them away the day before.

They seemed to be waiting for him and Kensa as they approached, and Toran stiffened. With the exception of one older woman, they all glared at Toran and Kensa with barely restrained hostility.

Kensa didn't show any hesitation, stopping before the witches and giving them all a respectful nod. One of the witches, another flame-haired woman who resembled the young witch who'd turned them away the day before, stepped forward, glowering at Kensa.

"My sister already told ye that we've nothing tae say tae ye. Go back tae yer own time."

Toran stepped forward before Kensa could reply. "I am a descendant of stiuireadh who perished at Tairseach," he said. "My family has long wanted tae ken what happened tae our ancestors, that is the only reason we're here in this time. 'Tis close tae the year 915, aye?"

Several of the witches seemed to hesitate at his words; he noticed their gazes all drift toward the older witch, who stood silently in the rear of the group.

"'Tis the year 917," the older witch replied.

He turned to look at Kensa at this confirmation, noting the relief on her face. They must be in the right time. He shifted his gaze to the baby in one of the witch's arms, determined to get the stiuireadh to warm up to him. He gave the child a smile. The baby cooed and returned it.

"Ah, the bairn reminds me of my grandson. Keep an eye on this one, he'll be a strong lad."

The young witch who held the baby looked at him with surprise, her gaze raking over him. "Ye're a grandfather?"

"Aye. With two grown sons around yer age. They also want tae ken what happened tae their ancestors," he said. "I assure ye that I'm honorable, as is Kensa. Ye can trust us both. We're staying at a cottage through the forest on the other side of the glen. That's where ye can find us when ye're ready."

He gave the witches another nod, and he and Kensa turned to walk away. He could feel the witches' eyes on them as they left.

They stopped at the small village market to purchase vegetables, bread, and salted herring before continuing on their way.

As soon as they were walking through the forest back toward the cottage, Kensa gave him an envious—but appreciative—look. "I should have let you do all the talking from the beginning," she said. "You at least got them to confirm what year we're in."

"They ken I'm nae a threat tae them. I have no magic."

"But they're still distrustful," Kensa mused. "What is it they're so afraid of?"

"I donnae ken. But they are afraid . . . of something. I could see it in their eyes."

Kensa paused and bit her lip. The action reminded him of how soft those lips had felt against his; he made himself avert his eyes from the tempting sight.

"If they refuse to give us any information, I'm not sure what to do. This year is the closest my magic has allowed me, and as far as I know, any stiuireadh to get to the time of the abandonment of Tairseach. I'm going to do a Seeking spell I prepared yesterday to see if I can find other stiuireadh from Tairseach, perhaps even other refugees who fled, nearby."

Pride swelled through him at the renewed determination in her eyes. He hadn't liked the frustration and self-doubt on her face the day before; she was a powerful witch and should have pride in her abilities.

"What?" she asked, catching his eye.

"I like seeing ye like this," he confessed. "Determined."

She returned his smile, which enhanced her lovely features, sending a rush of warmth through him.

When they returned to the cottage, he informed Kensa he could prepare their meal while she worked on her spells. Once she left, he prepared a stew made of the herring and vegetables they'd bought from the market; fish stew had been a favorite of his sons during the cold winter months when they were lads. He did his best to recreate Lyssa's recipe with the limited ingredients he had.

When Kensa returned and they sat down to eat, she let out a little moan that caused his arousal to stir as she took a bite of the stew. "This is delicious," she said.

"'Tis a favorite dish of my sons from when they were lads."

"You sound like an amazing father," she said, giving him a warm smile. "Even in my time it's not very common for men to cook for their sons."

"And yer father? Did he prepare meals for ye?"

"Neither of my parents were big cooks. They were too preoccupied with their magic, but they weren't neglectful. I was just as fascinated by all the things we could do as stiuireadh."

"It must have been a wonder," he mused, trying to imagine what it would be like to wield magic as a bairn.

"It was," Kensa said, her eyes filling with a look of nostalgia. "My parents taught me to treat magic and time travel as the great gift it was."

"Ye traveled through time when ye were a lass, aye?"

"Yes, but only with my parents. I didn't travel on my own until I was older."

"Where have ye gone during yer travels?" he asked, intrigued.

"Mostly to the past; travel to the future from the time you were born is possible, but more difficult. I've gone to times which still lie in the future for you: the Victorian era, pre-Revolutionary France, the Roaring Twenties."

She was right, those times sounded strange and foreign to him, but by the smile that tugged at her lips, he could tell she had enjoyed them. He realized with a pang of longing that he would have liked to see these times and places with her.

"We haven't gone anywhere notable in this time," she said, seeming to understand the look of longing in his eyes. "Maybe I can take you to see a landmark, something of note in this time."

"Learning what happened at Tairseach is our priority. Ye need nae take me tae see anything," he said, though he couldn't help but feel a twinge of excitement at her suggestion.

"We can spare an afternoon to do a little sightseeing," she said, her smile widening. At his look of confusion, she added, "Sightseeing is a common activity in my time. It's when you travel somewhere to take in historical or cultural sights for pleasure."

"I would like that," he said, excitement filling him once more. "Where will we go?"

"You'll see," Kensa replied, giving him a mischievous wink.

CHAPTER 7

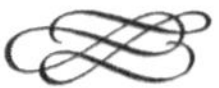

The next day, Kensa used a Transport spell to take them to the banks of Loch Ness. She'd decided to take him to the site of what would eventually become Urquhart Castle during his time—ruins and a popular tourist destination in her time—but now served as a fort. It was the closest she could get to showing him the effects of time travel, of seeing something before it existed in his own time.

When they arrived, Toran studied the looming fort in the distance, which bore little resemblance to the castle it would become, shaking his head in amazement.

"In four centuries that fort will become Urquhart Castle," she said, smiling at his awestruck reaction. She always took pleasure in the quiet awe of her travelers taking in the past, but for some reason she took particular delight in Toran's wonder.

"In my time, 'tis a full-fledged castle occupied by a powerful laird of the isles," Toran said. "Who dwells there now?"

"Now it's held by various local lords," Kensa said.

"What is it in yer time?"

"It's mostly in ruins. But many tourists—those are people who travel for leisure—come to visit it. I've been there in my own time and in the past," she said.

"Does it still fill ye with awe?" he asked, after a long pause. "Tae see things in varying stages in different times?"

"Yes," she said. "I may have gotten used to time travel, but there is something powerful about seeing the effects of time passing, something that most don't get to see."

They made their way to the nearby village where they purchased bread and ale from at the market before heading back to the banks of Loch Ness, sitting down to eat and taking in the natural beauty of their surroundings.

The shining waters of Loch Ness reflected the cloud-filled sky on its glimmering surface, birdsong filled the air, along with the clattering of horses as they made their way in and out of the fort in the distance. Rolling green hills and looming mountains bordered the vast emerald-green glen that surrounded the lake. Kensa took it all in for a moment, awestruck as always by the stunning beauty of the Highlands, no matter what era she was in.

As they ate, Toran asked her to describe in more detail some of the times she'd traveled to. She told him about witnessing the Industrial Revolution in its earliest forms during the Victorian era, the pomp and circumstance of eighteenth-century France, the opulence of the Roaring Twenties in the country that didn't yet exist in his time, but would become the United States.

"I am glad that I traveled for the first time with ye, Kensa," he said, when she finished. "But a part of me wishes I had used this ability sooner. I always put my duty first. 'Tis something my father instilled in me, duty above all else. He didnae care for the magic in my family's line. Said it was of the devil." His expression darkened when he mentioned his father. Catching her inquiring look, he continued, "My father was nae a kind man. He cared more for his lands and his duty than his own wife and son. 'Tis why I made certain tae be there for my sons. My sons and my late wife . . . they were my duty."

Kensa's chest tightened at the mention of his late wife, something she again chided herself for. "It's understandable why you chose your duty. Traveling through time . . . it's perilous. You had a family who needed you. And most importantly, you're doing it now."

"Aye," he said, and he reached out to take her hand, causing a spiral of heated awareness to career through her. "I thank ye, Kensa."

He held her gaze, and Kensa's heart raced as

she recalled the feel of his lips on hers, his hard muscular body pressed flushed against her, and an all-consuming ache filled her.

At that moment, she wanted nothing more than for him to lean forward, to seize her lips with his, to submit to the overwhelming desire that coursed through her . . .

But he dropped her hand, his expression heated yet unreadable, his gaze turning back to the lake.

The moment had passed, but Kensa's ache of desire remained.

THOUGH DESIRE still hummed between them, they fell into a routine over the next fortnight after returning from Loch Ness.

Kensa hoped that the witches from Ailin would come to them, but they did not, and she knew it would only arouse their hostility if she or Toran approached them again. So, in the mornings, she focused on issuing Seeking spells to try and locate other refugees from Tairseach after sharing a breakfast of porridge with Toran. Her Seeking spells didn't yield any results, yet she stubbornly persisted.

During one of her sessions in the forest clearing, she could have sworn she felt eyes on her, but when she looked up, no one was there. She dismissed it as heightened awareness, something that she was more prone to when she practiced her magic, though a lingering unease remained.

As for Toran, he had acclimated well to this time, and she felt ashamed for assuming a wealthy man such as himself couldn't adjust. While she worked on her spells, he took up chopping wood and hunting small game in the forest using tools stored away in the chest. Preparing and sharing meals with him became something she looked forward to; it distracted her from their lack of progress with the Tairseach mystery.

The undercurrent of desire between them still burned, yet they never acted on it or even mentioned the kiss, though the memory of it haunted Kensa: how good his body had felt against hers, the demand of his kiss, the powerful need for him that coursed throughout her body. She had to force herself to focus only on the growing friend-ship between them, relishing in getting to know the handsome man she was so wildly attracted to.

While his father had been cruel and died in battle against a rival clan, he spoke fondly of his mother, who had lived to old age, getting to meet his sons and Lyssa. Had it not been for her, he feared he would have inherited his father's coldness. He told her of his sons, of whom he was very proud, and their positions of respect among the clan as honorable men, something he also attributed to Lyssa's skills as a mother. Though she felt those ripples of jeal-ousy whenever he mentioned Lyssa, she noticed that he spoke of her the way one would speak of a close friend—with care and fondness, not with great passion or fervent love.

Or perhaps that was wishful thinking on her part.

As fascinated as she was about his life, he seemed even more fascinated by hers, asking about her family, her abilities, and her travels through time. To assuage his curiosity, she performed a spell for him as they took a walk through the forest one sunny afternoon.

"Stand back," she said, and he obliged, watching as she cast an Incendiary spell on the ground in front of her, before quickly dousing the flames it produced. He looked so wide-eyed with astonishment that she couldn't help but laugh.

"I take you back centuries to the past," she chided, "and you're in awe of this simple spell?"

"Aye," he said. "I donnae ken when I will get used tae it. I ken I've asked ye how it feels tae travel through time—and now I ken what that feels like. But what does it feel like when ye perform yer magic?"

She thought for a moment. Despite years of escorting people to the past, it wasn't a question she'd ever received before; she spent much of her non-traveling time with fellow stiuireadh.

"It's like . . . power humming beneath your skin. Pulling at you. And you get to control where it goes," she said. At his continued look of confusion, she added, "Like a group of horses tugging at you, but you can control them.

"Ah," he said, nodding. "How does this power work when ye bring lovers together?"

"That's more difficult to describe. My power helps me detect the two lovers who belong together. Love and desire—they're usually only tangible between two people. Like an invisible string that holds them together."

When her eyes met his, her pulse began to race, because she realized the tangible pull she felt toward Toran was the same. She could feel it now, like a string being pulled in the center of her chest, toward him . . . toward him . . . closer . . .

She didn't know which one of them moved forward first, but their lips were instantly pressed together, their arms winding around each other, and there wasn't a force in the universe that could tear them apart.

Toran's kiss was fervent and demanding; kissing him awakened the persistent ache between her thighs, and flames of desire seized her, entrapping her, surrounding her . . .

And then she sensed it.

Actual flames. Actual burning.

She pulled away from Toran, eyes wide, and turned in the direction of Ailin, where she heard distant screams.

A fire was ravaging the village. And though it was faint, Kensa could sense the taint of dark magic that was causing it.

CHAPTER 8

Kensa and Toran raced to the village, panic flaring in her gut. She still sensed that pervasive dark magic. Was a dark witch here in this time?

When they arrived in Ailin, it was in utter chaos. At least a dozen cottages and other small buildings were on fire, and men were rushing back and forth, using buckets of water to douse out the flames. Toran immediately sprang into action. "I'm going tae help put out the flames!" he shouted.

Kensa nodded, watching him join the men before racing to the edge of the village toward the coven's cottages.

She only found one of the witches there, the petite one with the baby, whom she rocked in her arms. She paced back and forth, her features frozen with shock. Kensa braced herself for the witch to tell her to leave, but instead she just gave her a blank, frozen look.

"Where are the others?" Kensa asked.

For a moment she thought the witch wouldn't respond, but she answered, her voice barely above a whisper. "They went tae the forest tae perform spells tae put out the fires. Their magic is stronger in the depths of the forest."

Kensa approached her cautiously. The baby smiled and cooed, reaching out his arms.

"What is your name?" she asked the young witch, smiling at the baby.

"Muire," she said absently.

Muire didn't react as Kensa took the baby from her arms, still looking dazed. *She's in shock*, Kensa realized. She looked down at the baby, who gave her a bright smile. Kensa returned it, settling the baby down into a surprisingly modern-looking cradle before turning to Muire.

"Muire," she said, holding her gaze. "You know this fire was caused by dark magic."

Muire flinched but said nothing. She wrapped her arms around herself and began to rock, tears streaming down her face.

Kensa studied her; wanting to keep questioning her, but she suspected it would only upset her more. She glanced at the doorway of the cottage. She wanted to help put out the fires, but she was reluctant to impede the magic the other witches were performing, and she could sense, and smell, that the fires were being carefully extinguished, through magical and non-magical means.

She decided to wait for the other witches to

return, moving to the cheerful baby's cradle and rocking it. She was prepared for their hostility, but this time she wouldn't back down. If there was indeed dark magic here in this time, she would help stamp it out, especially if it explained what had happened to Tairseach.

She didn't have to wait long. The first flame-haired witch who'd turned her away entered, trailed by the others. None of them look surprised to see her—they must have sensed her presence—yet their expressions were tight.

Kensa straightened to her full height, holding each of their gazes before she spoke. "That fire was caused by dark magic," Kensa stated.

The witches were silent for several long moments, until the flame-haired witch stepped forward. "Ye are the one who brought the dark magic here. They must have sensed ye're here. I told ye, go back tae yer own—"

"Eilys." It was the older witch who spoke now. She must have had some authority, because Eilys fell silent, though her eyes remained defiant.

The older witch stepped forward, offering Kensa a grave nod. "I am called Gormelia. I'm the leader of this coven," she said. "And aye. The attack was caused by *aingidh* using dark magic."

"Aingidh," Kensa echoed, a chill spreading down her spine. Aingidh were dark witches: stiuireadh who used their magic for malevolent purposes. "Were these dark witches responsible for Tairseach's abandonment?"

There was another long stretch of silence before Gormelia spoke.

"Aye," she confirmed. "Ye ken that powerful stiuireadh, direct descendants of the old druids, once lived in Tairseach."

Kensa nodded, and Gormelia continued, "The stiuireadh once lived in harmony until some of them wanted more power. They wanted tae twist our gift of traveling through time for their own selfish means. They killed innocents—and fellow stiuireadh—using their dark magic, and the other stiuireadh banished them for this, labeling them as aingidh for their actions. The aingidh took their revenge and attacked Tairseach, using the power of their newfound dark magic tae burn it tae the ground. Many stiuireadh who lived there were killed, though some managed tae escape. They scattered across the Highlands and tae other lands." She paused, meeting Kensa's eyes. "I'm one of them."

Sympathy swept over Kensa as she met Gormelia's eyes. It was all there in her haunted expression: the memory of the attack, her flight from Tairseach, her survivor's guilt. Perhaps it was because Gormelia was a fellow witch, but she could feel her pain as intensely as if it were her own.

"But the aingidh werenae done," Gormelia continued. "Dark magic had corrupted much of their power tae travel—many couldnae perform Time Weaving spells anymore. They began hunting down the stiuireadh who fled from

Tairseach, forcing them tae join them, tae use dark magic against their will. Those of us who joined covens or made new ones of our own were frightened and didnae trust outsiders. That's why we turned ye away," she continued, giving Kensa an apologetic look. "That's often how aingidh attack: they show up tae covens pretending tae be wayward travelers in need of help."

"What happened today?" Kensa pressed.

"We thought we were safe until today," Gormelia said, her face going pale. "We have a Cloaking spell around the village tae prevent any aingidh from tracking us. The fire was their way of breaking the spell. They now ken we're here. We stopped the fires, but now we must flee. The villagers ken we are descended from the old druids and they allow our presence here; many of them have druid blood themselves. We donnae want tae bring harm tae them. We will find somewhere else tae hide."

Kensa frowned. She had come here to find out what happened at Tairseach in the past, and now that she knew, she could leave. But her conscience wouldn't allow these witches to fend for themselves. The aingidh would keep seeking them out.

"I'm not here to do you harm. You can test me in any way you please to know I speak the truth. Now that I know what happened, I can help you. You must know the aingidh will keep pursuing you. I know spells, powerful spells, from a time yet to come. You need all the help you can get. Please . . . let me help you."

There was a pause. Gormelia turned to the other witches. A look of silent understanding seemed to pass between them, though some still looked reluctant. Kensa braced herself, expecting their refusal, but Gormelia gave her a warm smile.

"Verrae well, Kensa from a time yet tae come," said Gormelia. "We accept yer offer of help."

CHAPTER 9

Toran felt all eyes of the coven on him as he stood before Kensa, reeling from what he'd just learned.

He'd helped put out the fires with some male villagers, who were thankfully too distracted to question him about who he was or where he'd come from, though he had a story, with the help of Kensa, prepared. The fires had been surprisingly easy to put out; he suspected the coven must have worked their spells to quell the bulk of the fires from afar.

He'd come to the coven's main cottage, braced for Kensa to tell him they'd been turned away by the witches again. Instead, Kensa had approached him with a faltering smile and introduced to him by name each of the witches, who regarded him with wariness rather than outright hostility. She had then told him about the dark witches called aingidh who had caused the fire . . . and the abandonment of Tairseach.

He swallowed hard, trying to come to terms with all that Kensa had just told him. Even as someone who was aware of magic and time travel, he still found it difficult to comprehend. Dark witches? His great-grandmother had never mentioned such a thing. His heart clenched as he thought of how his ancestors must have suffered.

"Now that you know what happened at Tairseach," Kensa was saying gently, holding his gaze, "I can escort you back to your time. I'm going to stay here to help the coven fight the aingidh."

He blinked at her, his disbelief giving rise to anger and hurt. Did she really think he would just slink back to his own time now?

Yet in his gut, he knew she was right. He'd wanted to know what happened to Tairseach, and now he did. Still, he felt as if his time here wasn't yet complete. And, he had to admit to himself, he didn't want to leave without Kensa.

He straightened to his full height, meeting the gazes of all the witches before focusing on Kensa. He had the feeling that what he was going to say next would need the approval of them all.

"I ken I nae have magic," he said. "But I want tae stay. I can help in other ways."

"No," said Eilys, glaring at him. "This is a matter for the stiuireadh tae handle."

"My family perished at Tairseach," he said, returning her glare "'Tis my duty tae help fight."

"Yer sword and yer bravado are nothing to the

aingidh," Eilys hissed. "They have defeated witches more powerful than ye."

"I can help the villagers set up defenses," he returned. "I willnae leave until I've helped in some way tae defeat the dark witches who destroyed my ancestors."

There was a tense silence as he held himself rigid, prepared to fight for his right to stay in this time.

To his surprise, Kensa spoke up on his behalf. "I think he's right," she said. "If Toran wants to stay to help, we should allow him to do so."

Relief swept over him; he'd feared that she would insist he leave.

"Verrae well," Gormelia said. "Toran stays. We donnae have time tae argue amongst ourselves; there are more important matters at hand."

"I want you to tell us everything you know about these aingidh," Kensa said to the witches. "But first, let me help you create a more powerful Cloaking spell around the village to protect everyone."

"'Tis a wise plan," Gormelia said. "Ye can all go with Kensa. The spell will be stronger using the coven's collective magic. I wish tae stay behind and talk with Toran."

Surprise filled him; what could she want to discuss with him?

The witches and Kensa obliged her without question, though Kensa gave him a brief, concerned glance before leaving with the others.

"Toran," Gormelia said, when they were alone, gesturing for him to approach. "Come."

He wasn't used to someone ordering him around. In his own time, he held a leadership role in the clan and was beholden to no one but the chieftain. Yet there was something about the older witch that rang with authority, and he found himself approaching her without hesitation.

She studied him for a disconcertingly long moment before reaching out to grip his hands, closing her eyes. Instinct told him not to move; he remained still as her hands clutched his, her lips moving as she murmured words he could not understand beneath her breath.

When she opened her eyes once more, they were full of sorrow. "Ye are the kin of Cearach and Sibial. They lived in Tairseach," she said, her voice low, barely above a whisper.

"I kent of them," she continued, still speaking in that hushed tone as if she were in a trance. "Their power lay in the sensing of things tae come; they seemed tae ken that something dark was coming tae Tairseach. They could have fled, but they were loyal tae the coven; they wanted to protect the rest from what was tae come. They sent their two young sons, Naomhan and Iarlaith, away tae stay with non-magical relatives in the High- lands. 'Tis their blood that flows through yer veins."

Toran stared down at her, overwhelmed. Naomhan and Iarlaith. He had never heard the names before, but they reverberated with a familiarity down to his very soul. They were the ancestors who had survived Tairseach, whom he would descend from generations later.

He closed his eyes, a sense of peace settling over him. He hadn't realized how much he'd needed to know exactly what had happened to his ancestors until now. And though he wished they had all survived, gratitude coursed through him at the sacrifice that this Cearach and Sibial had made: a sacrifice that would allow him and his family line to exist.

"I thank ye," he said, his voice raspy with emotion. "'Tis what I have wanted tae ken for some time."

"I ken," she said, returning his smile. "I could see the longing in ye." She tilted her head to the side, studying him. "Ye want tae stay for more than just the avengement of yer ancestors. Ye wish tae stay with the lovely Kensa."

He stiffened. Was his desire for Kensa so obvious? Could Kensa tell as well?

Gormelia merely gave him a serene smile. "She cares for ye as well. Donnae allow her tae push ye away."

LATER THAT EVENING, Toran and Kensa sat in silence before the hearth in the cottage.

Kensa had spent the rest of the day with the witches, learning everything there was to know about these mysterious aingidh and teaching them spells from her own time to help protect both the coven and the village. Gormelia had taken Toran into the village and introduced him formally to some of the men with whom he'd helped put out the fires, telling them he would help erect a barrier around the village. Though magic could likely penetrate it, it would still create another needed layer of protection.

When he and Kensa had returned to the cottage after sharing dinner with the coven, he'd told her what he'd learned about his kin, and emotion had filled her eyes.

"I can't believe we're the only ones—as far as I know—to truly know what happened at Tairseach," Kensa said now, shaking her head.

"Aye," he agreed.

"They told me that the aingidh from Tairseach have only increased their numbers," she said with a sigh. "Toran, are you certain you want to stay in this time? Dark magic is dangerous. Me and the other stiuireadh can—"

"Aye," he said firmly. "I meant what I said. I willnae stand in the way of magic nor do anything foolish tae put myself in harm's way, but I will do what I can."

He took in Kensa's lovely features, recalling their kiss, the kiss the fire had interrupted.

He decided to tell her of his desire for her, consequences be damned—he was tired of fighting it. Gormelia's words echoed again in his mind. *Donnae allow her tae push ye away.*

He reached out to grasp Kensa's chin. Her eyes went wide with surprise, and he leaned in close, holding her gaze.

"And ye should ken . . . I donnae regret kissing ye. I will likely do it again," he said. He held her gaze for a long moment, allowing that imperceptible heat between them to flare, before murmuring, his words a husky promise, "Sleep well, lovely Kensa."

Kensa awoke the next morning on the heels of an erotic dream.

She'd never had an erotic dream before; Toran's husky words the night before had sent her spinning into sexual overdrive. It was hard to look at him as they shared breakfast, his words from the evening before still fresh in her mind. *I donnae regret kissing ye. I will likely do it again.*

It relieved her that they would spend the day apart. Kensa would work with the coven, training them in the more powerful spells from her time that they were unfamiliar with, along with Seeking and Tracking spells to try and locate the aingidh who had targeted them. Toran would join the men from the village, gathering wood from the forest to create a protective barrier that would surround the village.

This routine continued for the next week, with Kensa and Toran mostly spending their days apart as she worked with the coven and Toran with the male villagers. While Gormelia and several of the witches now treated her with polite friendliness, the others, including Eilys, continued to keep her at a distance.

She learned that Muire, the young witch with the baby, had lost her husband and the father of her child because of an aingidh. He'd sacrificed his life to protect his wife and child; Muire felt guilty to this day because she hadn't been able to save him.

Muire shakily explained to Kensa that her shock during the fires caused by the aingidh came from a paralyzing fear that they would harm her child.

Sympathy roiled through Kensa, and she placed her hand over hers. "I will do whatever I can to protect you and this coven from the dark witches. But I also believe you are stronger than you realize, and you're more than capable of protecting both yourself and your child."

Muire had given her a tremulous smile, and after that moment, she treated her with just as much warmth as Gormelia did.

It turned out it was more than just Muire who'd suffered losses at the hands of the aingidh. Eilys, the witch who had initially turned them away, and Ceitidh, her sister, had lost both their parents the year before to an aingidh who'd pretended to be a wayward traveler in need of help. Now she understood their continued distance and wariness; it would take time to earn their trust.

She also learned that it was Gormelia whose eyes she'd felt watching her in the forest clearing while she'd performed Seeking spells.

"I wanted tae make certain ye were nae an aingidh," Gormelia explained. "I sensed ye had a good heart, but I needed tae be sure ye werenae deceiving us. I was going tae approach ye on my own, but then the fire happened, and ye came tae us as I'd hoped ye would."

"Thank you for telling me," Kensa said. "And for trusting me. Given what you and your coven have gone through with the aingidh, I don't blame you for your initial mistrust."

A brief pause stretched before Gormelia spoke once more. "I ken that this isnae my concern, but I would urge ye," she said, "tae nae hold back on yer feelings for Toran. I see the way he looks at ye."

Kensa froze, taken aback. Embarrassment flooded her, and she swallowed hard. "Gormelia, Toran and I are staying in this time together to help you stop the aingidh and nothing more. I've long since accepted that magic is the guiding force in life, nothing else." But even to her own ears, her words sounded hollow and unconvincing.

"Is love so different from magic? As someone who has linked souls across centuries, ye should ken that."

Gormelia left before Kensa could respond, joining the witches in the clearing as they practiced Defensive and Offensive spells that Kensa had taught them.

Kensa clenched her fists at her side, her pulse thrumming. Did Gormelia think she was in love with Toran? She ached with desire for Toran, but she didn't love him. She hadn't even known him for very long. If she loved him, she would certainly know. *It's just desire*, she told herself firmly. *Just desire, and desire can be quelled.*

But as the days wore on, her desire for him became more and more difficult to dismiss. She found herself looking forward to their walks in the forest when they would leave the village and head back to their cottage, and their dinners during which they spoke of their day, and their lives in their own time, before retreating to their own beds.

She noticed that the ache that persisted between her thighs as she fell asleep on her bed pallet seemed to affect her heart as well. If she were in a battle with her need for Toran, she was losing. Badly.

The next evening, as they walked back to the cottage from the village, Kensa's heart hammered violently against her chest at Toran's proximity. Even in the worn tunic he wore, he looked impossibly handsome, his silver-streaked dark hair now long enough to brush against his shoulders, and he now sported a full beard. He smelled of earth and woodsmoke, his masculinity as potent as his male beauty.

He was telling her about a friendship he was forging with a man from the village and his young sons as they erected the barrier around the village, and how it reminded him of his relationship with his own sons. She was trying to concentrate on his words, she really was, but she found her gaze lingering on his wide, sensual mouth, the sparkle of his gray eyes. Why did he have to be so distractingly handsome? Why did he have to possess such honor, such inherent goodness? Why did his very presence make her heart palpitate in a way it never had before?

He abruptly stopped in his tracks, reaching out to grab her hand, and a jolt of electricity tore through her. He was gesturing up at the sky, where an opening in the trees revealed a multitude of stars.

"'Tis lovely," he murmured, and she nodded in agreement, taking in the dazzling array of stars.

She felt his gaze on her face and turned to meet his eyes. They were filled with desire as they raked over her, and her heartbeat skyrocketed.

As he leaned in toward her, she realized that she was tired of fighting her desire, her need for him. She had traveled through time; she had fought against dark magic and the witches who wielded it, yet she was powerless to resist her pull toward this man.

And so she gave in, meeting the demand of his kiss with a fierce need of her own.

CHAPTER 11

As Toran's mouth probed hers, Kensa was so swept up in a torrent of desire that she barely noticed when he lifted her up into his arms, carrying her the rest of the way to the cottage.

He reluctantly tore his lips away as he walked with her in his arms as if she weighed nothing, and when they arrived in the cottage, he set her down on her feet, looking at her with eyes that burned with need.

"I ache for ye, sweet Kensa," he rasped. Kensa flushed as his eyes roamed her face, dipping down to her bosom, the swell of her hips. Never had a man looked at her that way, as if he hungered for her; she'd assumed that once she grew older, no man ever would.

"Men in my time often prefer younger women," she whispered, and he gave her a look of disbelief.

"The men in yer time are fools," he muttered,

and once again leaned in to seize her mouth with his.

Kensa wrapped her arms around him, her hunger for him consuming every inch of her. He moaned into her mouth before pulling back.

"I need tae undress ye," he whispered, and taking her hand, he pulled her before the hearth which she lit with a quickly murmured Incendiary spell.

His eyes burned on her skin as he reached out to strip her of her gown, slowly, as if he were unwrapping a most precious present. His expression sharpened with desire as his eyes raked over her nude form, and he let out a low growl as he again leaned forward to seize her mouth with his.

Her nipples hardened against his muscular torso; she pressed herself against him, moisture seeping between her thighs as her need for him consumed her, an all-encompassing voracity that she had never felt before.

Toran released her and began to disrobe. Kensa took him in, her mouth watering as her gaze drank in his masculine beauty—the muscular breadth of him, the size of him. Her gaze lingered on his groin, and she almost felt like a frightened virgin again.

Toran reached out to cup her chin, lifting her face to meet his. "I will be gentle," he said, his eyes infused with a teasing glint. "At first."

She expelled a breath at his words, and he claimed her mouth with his, gripping her buttocks to lift her up as he moved with her over to his bed pallet. Kensa wrapped her legs around him, feeling his need for her pressed against her belly, and she whimpered with anticipated pleasure.

He laid her down carefully onto the pallet, his eyes raking over every inch of her nude skin. Keeping his eyes locked with hers, he leaned down to seize one aching nipple into his mouth, and then the other. She groaned, tossing her head back as he suckled upon her, electricity buzzing through her at the pleasure his mouth evoked.

He continued lower, peppering kisses along her skin, lower still, and she gasped, arching against him as his mouth clamped onto her center, his tongue dipping and probing into her body, causing her to clench around him, ripples of pleasure consuming her until a climax tore through her, causing her body to shake and convulse as she cried out.

He kept his mouth clamped onto her, and her hands lowered to his hair as he continued to plea-sure her, her body still quavering with aftershocks until she went still. Only then did he remove his mouth from her center.

He hovered above her, his eyes raking over her form. "Bonnie Kensa," he rasped, "ye're even more lovely when yer release claims ye. I intend tae get many more releases from ye before the sun rises."

Kensa moaned at his words, her gaze locking with his as he entered her in one smooth thrust. Despite his height, their bodies fit perfectly together, and she locked both her arms and legs around him as he began to move, his body pounding against hers in that age-old rhythm.

"Look at me, sweet Kensa," he whispered as she closed her eyes, the pleasure almost too much to bear. "I want tae see yer lovely eyes as I fill ye with my seed."

The words alone caused even more spikes of pleasure to pierce her. She obliged, opening her eyes as she arched against him, and he let out a groan as a torrential climax claimed them both, their bodies quaking together.

When they stilled, Toran gave her a wicked grin, kissing the side of her neck, her breasts, her stomach, lower still . . .

"I told ye I will give ye more releases before the sun rises," he whispered. "I always keep my promises, sweet Kensa."

And Kensa let out a cry as his mouth once again found her center.

Later, much later, they held each other, panting and out of breath.

Kensa buried her head into his neck. He'd wrung two more orgasms from her with his mouth before making love to her again, leaving her weak with pleasure. Never had she experienced such intense passion, never had such desire consumed her.

It's more than desire. I love him.

The realization struck her with the force of a sledgehammer. How had Gormelia seen it before she had? How had she not seen it, when she had brought together so many lovers through the veil of time? She craved more than just Toran's handsome body; she craved his company, sharing meals and walks with him, discussing the magic and beauty of time travel . . . sharing everything with him. Seeing him that first time at Diana and Artair's manor had been like her soul recognizing its other half. She'd witnessed it countless times when she'd brought lovers together, smiling as she watched them from afar.

Now it had happened to her.

But what to do with this knowledge? Toran had a life in his own time, and even though his sons were adults and his wife long gone . . . what if his late wife still had his heart? How could Kensa compete with that? Even if she could, would Toran want someone like her for a companion? A time-traveling witch who rarely stayed in the same place —the same time—for long?

"Sweet Kensa," Toran said, pulling her from the torrent of her thoughts, "what ails ye? Did I nae give ye enough pleasure? Do ye need more?" He gave her a sexy, teasing grin, running his fingers up and down her body, leaving a trail of electricity along with his touch.

Oh, nothing. I just realized that I'm in love for the first time in my life, something I assumed would never happen, she thought, her heart pounding violently in her chest. *That you are what I've been looking for without even realizing it. And I don't know if you feel the same.*

But she said none of this. Instead, she returned his smile with a teasing one of her own. "I don't think I can take any more pleasure. I don't know if you could tell, but it's been quite a while for me."

Toran scowled, and she realized with a flare of delight that jealousy lurked in his gaze. "Toran . . . I've never experienced pleasure like I have tonight."

Her words seemed to quell his jealousy, and he smiled. He reached up to cup her face, gazing at her with such intensity that her breath hitched. "Nor have I, sweet Kensa." His expression suddenly changed, and he pulled back, his gaze raking over her face with puzzlement. "Kensa—yer face has changed."

Kensa froze, reaching up to touch her face. It felt smoother, more youthful.

She flushed with embarrassment. A side effect of her magical abilities was something called *aosu tapa*, an aging and de-aging process that could make her look older or younger. It usually happened right after she performed a powerful spell. Given how closely her magic was entwined with her emotions, it made sense that her magic would react in some way to the intense passion she'd just experienced.

When she explained to Toran what it was, he looked utterly fascinated, shaking his head with amazement.

"You get used to it," she said. "Just a side effect of having magic."

"'Tis a wonder what ye can do, Kensa."

He gave her a look that was full of pride, and Kensa's heart swelled. Surrounded by fellow witches for most of her life, no one took much pride in their powers: they were considered commonplace. Seeing magic through Toran's eyes was refreshing.

Toran held her close, and they spoke more of the wonder of magic and time travel as they drifted off to sleep. Sleep claimed Toran first, and she listened to the steadiness of his breathing as he slept. She curled against him, closing her eyes. *How I love this man*, she thought with a surge of joy. *I don't want to hide it. I'm going to tell him how I feel as soon as we wake tomorrow.*

Toran began to shift, as if in the middle of a restless dream, and murmured, "Lyssa . . ."

Kensa froze, her heart splintering in her chest. Lyssa. His first wife, whom he was dreaming of after making love to her.

Moisture brimmed in her eyes, jealousy and heartbreak piercing her. While it was love for her, it was just desire for Toran. She should have realized that. He had shared decades with Lyssa. Sons. His heart would always belong to her.

What had she been thinking? Kensa was the opposite of everything he'd had with Lyssa: stability, normalcy. Even if she stopped traveling, Kensa was and always would be a stiuireadh.

Kensa blinked back her tears, lifting her head from his chest. She sat up, tugging on her under-dress, and moved over to her bed pallet.

She knew what she had to do next. She just hoped that she could go through with it, despite her aching heart.

CHAPTER 12

Toran awoke slowly, snatches of his dream lingering in his mind.

The images from his dream were still vague, but he could clearly recall one distinct part. He'd seen Lyssa, looking just as she had before she'd died. She'd stood before him in a clearing, much like the clearing Kensa often practiced her spells in, giving him a patient smile.

As he'd gazed at her, he felt no great longing, no desire, no love. Not even sadness. He'd realized in that moment that what he'd felt for Lyssa paled in comparison to what he felt for Kensa, whom he'd only known for a short time but felt as if he'd known much longer. For the first time, he felt . . . complete with another person. Making love to her had been the most natural thing in the world.

No guilt struck him at the realization, only joy. Joy that at long last, he'd found the woman meant for him. As he'd gazed at the dream Lyssa, he felt the need to apologize to her. They had been dear friends, and she was the mother of his sons.

"Lyssa . . ." he'd begun to say, but dream Lyssa had only held up her hand, her smile widening.

"There is no need tae apologize, Toran. Ye were a good husband tae me, a good father tae our sons. Ye deserve happiness and love."

Now, a sense of peace settled over him as he recalled dream Lyssa's words. *Love.* Aye, he was in love with the bonnie witch, and he was going to tell her. He didn't know if she would want to anchor herself to someone non-magical such as himself, but he would happily travel to any time or place with her, as long as he could be by her side.

He turned to his side, reaching for her, but she wasn't there. He frowned, sitting up. She wasn't in the other bed pallet either.

Dread coiled around his body. Did she regret what had happened between them? Should he have held back?

No. There had been no denying her response to him—she was hungry, eager. He hardened at the memory of how she'd arched against him, how she'd cried out his name after her final release.

He quickly got dressed and headed to the village, making his way to the coven's cottages. He found her behind the main cottage with Gormelia, Eilys, Muire, and several other witches, demonstrating Defensive spells. If she noticed him, she gave no indication, though he noticed her shoulders stiffen.

"Practice on your own. I'll be back shortly," she told Gormelia and the others.

She approached, not looking directly at him as she headed into the empty cottage. He trailed her inside, unease filling his belly. This was not the warm, passionate woman he'd made love to last night. This was a stranger.

"Toran," she said, once they were inside, looking at some point past his shoulder. "The other witches and I are concerned that the aingidh will return in greater numbers. It's too dangerous for you to remain in this time."

Disbelief, hurt, and confusion flooded him. Kensa was still not looking at him, and continued, "I'll help escort you back to your own time, of course."

"Kensa . . ." he rasped, stepping forward, praying that she would look at him. "Kensa, please. Look at me. What is it? Do ye regret last night?"

Kensa met his gaze, and the coldness in her eyes struck him like an arrow. It was as if last night, or the past few weeks, had never happened, and he was looking at a stranger.

"Yes," she said stiffly. "It—it shouldn't have happened."

"Ye donnae mean that," he hissed, taking another step forward. She stepped back, and he could have sworn he saw a flash of despair in her eyes before it vanished.

"I do," she said firmly. "It shouldn't have happened. I—I should have insisted that you leave once you found out what happened to your ancestors. There's nothing further between us. It's time for you to return."

As he gazed at the woman he loved, grief and heartbreak splintered his chest. How could he have thought that such a creature as she, a mystical, time-traveling witch, would want to tie herself to him? She desired him, aye, there was no denying her response to him last night. But she wanted nothing more, and he had too much pride to beg a woman who did not want him.

"Verrae well," he said shortly. "I'll return tae the cottage. When ye're done here, ye can escort me back tae my own time."

Again, there was that flash of despair in her eyes before it disappeared. She gave him a curt nod, turning around and heading back outside.

Toran watched her go, clenching his fists at his sides, forcing himself to remain where he was, to not chase after her and demand to know if she felt anything for him. Yet pride hardened his heart, and he turned to leave the cottage.

As he made his way through the forest on the way back to the cottage, he had to force himself to not think of the warm, passionate woman he'd made love to last night, and the cold woman who'd just sent him away. It was as if they were two different people . . . but they weren't. They were both his sweet Kensa, the woman he loved. The woman he would always love, despite her rejection.

He made his way to the creek they'd come to after they first arrived in this time, but for once the sound of rushing water over rocks didn't bring him calm. It just reminded him of Kensa's smile, her laughter, her beauty. Everything reminded him of Kensa.

Toran abruptly stilled when he sensed another presence in the forest. Heart thundering, he looked up as several people emerged from the clearing behind him—two women and a man. Though they wore clothing of this time, simple tunics and gowns, there was something different about them.

He didn't know how he knew, but he suspected they weren't human. They were witches. And they didn't have the benign air of the other witches he'd met with Kensa. Malevolence seemed to drip from their skin.

"Ah," said one of the women, a dark-haired lass with sharp green eyes that seemed to pierce right through him. Like her presence, her voice seemed to echo with a darkness, an evil that shaped every word. "The stiuireadh from a time yet tae come has brought us a gift. He shall be our sacrifice and lure her tae us."

Panic swept over him, and he stumbled back, prepared to run. But the dark-haired witch was before him in an instant. Despair gripped him as he realized that this dark witch could be the last person he ever saw—not his sons, nor his Kensa. He cried out for them all in his heart as the dark witch placed her hand on his arm, her green eyes seeming to burn into him as she uttered a spell.

Iain. Caomhain. Kensa. I love ye all, he thought, with a wave of grief and regret.

And then darkness claimed him.

CHAPTER 13

After Toran left, Kensa hovered behind the witches as they practiced the spells she had taught them. She fought to keep her expression neutral, though her heart was breaking, and she had to continually blink back tears.

It had taken everything in her power to not break down in front of Toran, to not tell him she loved him. But she had clung to the walls she'd erected around her heart, determined to not let them shatter. She had gone all her life without love; she would endure. She had to.

Yet the thought of never seeing Toran again made grief sweep over her.

"I overheard yer talk with Toran," Gormelia said.

Kensa started; the older witch had appeared at her side out of nowhere. Gormelia had a habit of sneaking up on her when she least expected it.

She stiffened as Gormelia's words struck her;

she'd listened in on her private conversation with Toran. Kensa tried to feel righteous anger over the breach of her privacy, but her heartache left no room for anything else besides a dull ache.

"It was for the best," Kensa said stiffly, watching as Muire successfully landed an Offensive spell against a tree.

"And why is that?" Gormelia pressed.

Kensa gritted her teeth, tempted to politely but firmly tell Gormelia that it was none of her business. When she turned to Gormelia to do just that, she was looking at Kensa with such empathy that her defiance melted away. Kensa expelled a sigh and closed her eyes, fighting another wave of tears.

"Toran and I . . ." she began, hesitant to divulge the intimate details of her night with Toran.

"Ye made love," Gormelia finished for her.

Embarrassment flooded Kensa, but she gave Gormelia a jerky nod. As a matchmaker she wasn't necessarily opposed to discussing sex, but it wasn't easy discussing her own intimacy. She forced herself to continue, feeling the sudden need to confide in someone.

"Yes," she said. "And afterward . . . afterward, he said his late wife's name in his sleep." Her voice broke at the memory, and pain pierced her once more.

To her surprise, Gormelia wasn't giving her a look of sympathy or understanding. Instead, she looked at her with disapproval.

"Ah, Kensa," she said with a sigh. "As a matchmaker ye should ken that things are nae always what they seem."

"Toran saying his late wife's name in his sleep after making love to me is exactly as it seems," Kensa returned sharply, though doubt was already beginning to stir in her gut.

"Do ye love him?" Gormelia asked, leveling her with a hard stare.

"Yes," Kensa said without hesitation. There was no use denying it; Gormelia had sensed her love for Toran before she had.

"And have ye ever loved anyone else?"

"No," she whispered, her heart clenching.

"Ye ken more than anyone how precious and rare love is, how it must be fought for. Ye've fought for love for others, now is the time tae fight for yer love. I urge ye tae talk tae him."

Kensa weighed Gormelia's words. Toran had looked hurt when she'd sent him away. Yet she'd definitely heard his late wife's name on his lips last night.

Perhaps there was a reasonable explanation? His speaking her name didn't have to mean that he still loved Lyssa . . . or that he didn't love Kensa. Perhaps her insecurity over his past marriage had made her leap to conclusions.

Kensa swallowed hard, her heart picking up its pace as she made a decision. She would talk to Toran and tell him she loved him. If her initial conclusion was right, and there was indeed no room in his heart for her, at least she would have told him how she felt. At least she would have had the experience of loving him . . . even if she couldn't have him, even if him not loving her in return would shatter her. She just knew that if she didn't talk to him, she would forever regret it.

"Go," Gormelia urged her, seeming—as always—to read her mind. "Talk tae the man ye love."

"I will," Kensa said, giving her a tremulous smile. She glanced outside to where the witches were practicing, but Gormelia waved her away. "I can watch over them until ye return."

Kensa nodded her thanks and turned to leave the cottage, her pulse thrumming with nervous anticipation.

For the first time in her life, she was going to tell a man she loved him. And maybe, just maybe, he would tell her he loved her in return. A smile curved her lips at the thought, but before she could even step out of the cottage, a terrible pain tore through her body, like liquid fire racing through her veins. She gasped and stumbled to her knees.

This was no ordinary, physical pain. It was caused by magic—by dark magic. She knew it in her bones. She heard an unintelligible whisper in her mind, and then images of Toran's battered face and body.

He was lying in a clearing, surrounded by witches. The aingidh. With terrible clarity, she knew exactly what she was experiencing. A Summoning spell. A Summoning spell from the aingidh . . . and they had Toran.

CHAPTER 14

Kensa didn't realize she was crying out until she felt Gormelia's arms around her.

"Kensa! Kensa! What is it?" Gormelia asked, her tone frantic.

Kensa looked up, panic and fear surging through her veins. She noticed that the other witches were now gathered around as well, looking at her with concern.

"A Summoning spell was just used on me—it's tainted with dark magic. It's the aingidh," she rasped. "They have Toran. I need to go to him—now!"

She stumbled to her feet, but Gormelia reached for her, holding her firm. "No, Kensa."

"Did you not hear me?" Kensa hissed. "The aingidh have Toran—I saw him. He's hurt, and—"

"Why do you think they sent you those images? This is what they want. If ye go tae them alone, the aingidh will overpower and destroy ye, and then ye and Toran will be lost. We will come with ye, but we must prepare. With the power of our collective magic and the new spells ye've taught us, we can stop them."

"I can't lose him," Kensa said, tears stinging her eyes.

"I ken," Gormelia returned, reaching out to cup her face. "We will find him and stop the aingidh—together."

〜

Kensa's heart hammered violently against her rib cage as she arrived in the center of a large, sprawling glen.

It was just after midday; she and the coven had worked tirelessly during the past few hours to prepare several powerful group spells to use against the aingidh. They had then prepared a Cloaking spell to hide behind so the rest of the coven could remain undetected when Kensa heeded the Summoning spell and approached the aingidh.

It had been difficult to focus as she worked with the coven, her worried thoughts centered on Toran and the images of his bruised and battered body.

If only I hadn't sent him away. If only I'd told him I loved him.

But she had no time to linger on her feelings of regret. She had to focus on preparing her magic to fight the aingidh; it was the only way she could save him.

Once she and the coven had finished their magical preparations, Kensa performed a Linking spell to join her power with the coven's and heeded the pull of the Summoning spell sent by the aingidh, allowing it to apparate her and the coven to this glen.

Now, she looked around, fear and unease slithering through her. She couldn't tell exactly where she was, but given the surrounding mountains and glen with no hint of dirt roads or villages nearby, she suspected she was deep in the Highlands.

Gormelia and the coven were a dozen yards behind her, hidden beneath the Cloaking spell. Though she knew she was not alone, she still had to struggle to contain her anxiety. She had fought against dark magic before, but it had been long ago; she was inherently not a fighter, preferring to use her magic for benevolent purposes rather than to harm, even if it was for self-defense.

Yet for Toran, she would fight a million battles.

She looked around the empty glen. *Where are you, Toran?* She issued a silent Summoning spell of her own and images immediately flooded her mind; Toran keeled over in pain, gasping for breath.

Anguish tore at her; he was nearby. *I will rescue you, my love,* she silently pledged. *Hold on.*

She took a breath, extending her arms, and in the most powerful voice she could muster, she said, "I am called Kensa, stiuireadh from a time yet to come. I have heeded your Summoning. Reveal yourself to me."

For several moments there was nothing but silence and the whisper of the breeze. And then, a sense of darkness and dread swept over her as one by one, a half-dozen aingidh appeared before her—along with Toran.

To her horror, they surrounded the man she loved. He was on his knees, keeled over in pain, his dark hair covering his handsome face, his breathing ragged.

On instinct she stumbled toward him, but a spell instantly repelled her backward. Kensa fell to her knees, gasping as the air was temporarily knocked from her lungs.

One of the aingidh, a dark-haired woman with cold green eyes, stepped forward and spoke. "Tell the other witches ye have hidden away beneath yer Cloaking spell tae leave, or we will kill him."

Terror gripped Kensa. By the deadly look in her eyes, Kensa could tell the witch was serious. Panicked, she stumbled to her feet and turned to face Gormelia and the witches hidden from view by the Cloaking spell.

"Leave," she said. "Please."

There was silence, but she could sense the witches' resistance through the Linking spell that bonded them. *Please*, she urged, through their bond. *I will fight them alone. They will kill Toran if you don't leave.*

After several tense beats, the Cloaking spell fell

away, briefly revealing Gormelia and the witches. They all looked torn and reluctant to leave her, but they vanished as quickly as they'd appeared. Once she knew they were gone, she turned back to face the aingidh.

"We are alone now. Please let him go," she said, trying to keep her voice firm. "It is me you want—my power, my magic. He is of no use to you; he has no magic. Let him leave and you can have me."

The aingidh tilted her head to the side. "Ye will sacrifice yerself for this *salachar?*"

Kensa flinched at the word, a slur that the aingidh used for those without magic. "Yes," she said, and realized that she meant it. She would do anything for Toran to survive, to get back to his time and live, even if they couldn't be together. Even if it meant her own life. She loved him that much.

"Who are you? Why are you doing this?" she continued, needing to keep the witch talking. She had to get Toran clear of the witches before she attempted a Killing spell on them.

"I am called Fiadha. I was once a stiuireadh of the ancient village of the druids, Tairseach. I wanted the stiuireadh tae use their power tae make all of us stronger, so that we donnae have tae live in hiding from the salachar because of their greater numbers. Yet I and my brethren were cast aside and called aingidh, dark ones, for our desire to strengthen our magic. Aye, we were willing tae use the dark tae sacrifice both the blood of witches and the salachar. But it was necessary tae protect ourselves and our power. Ye are from a time yet tae come, ye ken what humans will do tae witches, tae those they fear. We are greater than humans. Using our power, what we ken of time, we can have them living in fear of us."

"You must know that we bend to the will of time, not the other way around," Kensa pleaded. "We can only change what time dictates to us to change. Such power is delicate, it is why only a few of us wield it."

"*We* manipulate time," Fiadha hissed. "We have power over it and all the elements of nature. And now, we will use the blood of stiuireadh such as yerself tae strengthen our magic. I can sense yer power, the amount of time ye have traveled through. I sensed yer presence here in this time, soon after I found the weak coven ye're trying tae protect. I no longer have need of them . . . yer magic is stronger. Ye will make us stronger. Ye are a gift that time has brought tae us."

Kensa stared at the dark witch, chilled. She could see the hunger for power in her eyes, the all-encompassing darkness. Fiadha was lost; there was no hope in reaching her with reason.

"Please, let him go, and you have my willing sacrifice. Your magic will be more potent if you have a willing participant. You said you sensed how great my power is. Take it, but let Toran go. He is of no use to you."

The dark witch turned to face the other

aingidh, and they seemed to come to a mutual decision. To Kensa's relief, one of the aingidh jerked Toran to his feet, shoving him forward.

Toran stumbled toward her, and she wrapped her arms around him, needing to take him in, if only for a moment. The dark witches had bruised his handsome face, but his gray eyes were still sharp as they met hers.

"Toran," she whispered, knowing that these may very well be the last words she ever spoke to him if she failed in what she was about to do. "I love you. Now I need you to run."

Emotion filled his eyes. He swayed against her, his jaw tightening. "I willnae leave the woman I love," he rasped.

Kensa's heart swelled, but there was no time for joy. Fiadha and the other aingidh were focused intensely on them; it was only a matter of time before they struck.

"And I will not let the man I love die," she returned.

She moved quickly, uttering a Protective spell that surrounded Toran, and then she launched herself forward, shouting a Killing spell.

"*Marbh an stiuireadh seo!*"

Fiadha and the other aingidh were prepared for her, and sent her hurtling back with an Offensive spell. In an instant they were surrounding her—and Toran. Terror tore through her; they were going to kill them both.

Her eyes met Toran's. *I'm sorry. I love you.* He

seemed to understand, his eyes filling with a torrent of emotions, and as the aingidh raised their arms to issue a collective spell—

Gormelia, Eilys, and the other witches from the coven appeared around them. They began to chant, in unison, the Killing spell that Kensa had taught them.

Kensa stumbled to her feet, reaching Toran and pushing him protectively behind her as she joined in with the chant.

"Sgrios olc nan aingidh seo . . . Sgrios olc nan aingidh seo . . ."

The aingidh were trying to issue counterspells of their own, but the strength of Kensa and the coven's spell overpowered them.

Fiadha and the other aingidh sank to the ground, their cries of agony rising as their bodies writhed in pain before dissolving into nothing, leaving behind only the echo of their screams.

CHAPTER 15

It took a full fortnight for Toran to heal, as he was still in a great deal of pain. His time with the aingidh was hazy; he remembered them surrounding him, and then searing pain as they uttered spells and curses that struck his face and body. As he'd drifted in and out of consciousness, powerless to defend himself against their magic, he prayed he would survive to see his sons again . . . to see Kensa again.

When he'd come to in the glen and seen her, fierce and brave as she faced off with the aingidh who'd kept him captive, the pride, relief, and love he'd felt had nearly overwhelmed him.

After she and the other witches had destroyed the aingidh, she'd rushed to his side and pulled him into her arms, murmuring words of love which he'd returned, clinging to her and never wanting to let her go, even as his body ached.

When they returned from the glen, Kensa and

the others settled him in at Gormelia's cottage, where they tended to him with Healing spells and drafts, feeding him hot broth and vegetable stew. It was mostly Kensa who tended to him, and he tried to stay conscious whenever she was at his side, but fatigue kept claiming him, and she insisted that he needed to heal.

After a few days he was well enough to stay awake throughout the day, and a reluctant Kensa allowed him to take brief walks through the nearby forest.

"Why did ye try tae send me away?" he asked her during one of their walks.

It was something that lingered in his mind and still troubled him even though he knew she loved him; her risking her life to rescue him had proved her love beyond a doubt.

"I was hurt . . . and jealous," Kensa said, after a brief pause, her face flushing. "I heard you say your late wife's name in your sleep after we made love and . . . it shattered me. I thought your heart still belonged to her. And if it does, it's all right," she added quickly, not looking at him, though he noticed her body tensed at her words. "I just—"

"Kensa," Toran interrupted, turning her to face him. "I donnae love Lyssa. I cared for her deeply, and she was a good mother tae our sons. But we never had great love nor passion for each other. I've only ever experienced that with ye. When ye heard me say her name, I did see her in my dream, aye— but it was because I wanted tae apologize tae her for nae loving her. She told me I deserved happiness."

Kensa's eyes filled with emotion, and she swallowed hard. "I was a fool," she whispered. "And to think that I almost lost you."

"Ye didnae," he fiercely returned. "And ye never will. Back at the glen, with those dark witches—I would have gladly died for ye if it meant sparing yer life."

"I only want you to live for me," she murmured, and he leaned forward to kiss her, their hearts thundering together as he held her close.

When he released her, he said, "Remember when ye told me about that word—exhilaration? Ye described it as a joy so complete it almost takes your breath away."

"Yes," she said, smiling, still breathless from his kiss. "I remember."

"That is how ye make me feel, sweet Kensa," he said. He gripped her hand, nervousness filling him, but he needed to ask her this. He needed her at his side—always. "I ken I donnae have magic. And I ken ye're a stiuireadh, and ye've never had need nor want for a husband. But I want ye tae be my wife. I want tae travel with ye . . . I want tae always be at yer side. I've gone my whole life without ye, and I donnae want tae spend a moment more without ye."

Tears brimmed in Kensa's eyes. She reached up to cup his face.

"Yes, Toran," she said. "You are the only man I

have ever and will ever love. Some part of me knew it the moment I laid eyes on you. I want to spend the rest of my life with you."

Joy surged through Toran, and despite his lingering weakness, he picked Kensa up and swung her around. She laughed as he set her down, pulling her close for another searing kiss.

They returned to the coven, telling Gormelia and the others about their engagement. The witches reacted with joy, and even Eilys and Ceitidh congratulated them.

Gormelia embraced them both, tears of joy brimming in her eyes. "I ken ye two belonged together," she whispered. "After witnessing such darkness with the aingidh, it is good tae see such love."

They shared a final meal with the coven before they left, with Kensa inquiring about Tairseach and what would happen to it now that they'd destroyed the aingidh.

"We still cannae return there tae live; 'tis been tainted by dark magic. But the deaths of those aingidh have purified it. It will continue as a time travel gateway for generations to come," Gormelia replied.

"What about other aingidh?" Kensa asked, looking worried.

"Evil will always exist, in any time, but we have destroyed the most powerful of the aingidh here in this time. With the spells ye have taught us from a time yet tae come, we can protect ourselves. Ye need nae worry about us, Kensa. Ye and Toran have done more than enough tae help us."

Later, Kensa and Toran bade farewell to the coven and returned to their own cottage, where they spent their last night in the tenth century making love and discussing plans for their future.

They decided that they would make their semi-permanent home in Toran's time because of the presence of his sons and her niece, Diana, but Toran would accompany Kensa on her travels to different times, which they both looked forward to.

"It doesnae matter tae me where we go, or when," Toran whispered, after they made love a second time, their bodies entwined. "As long as I'm with ye."

LESS THAN A MONTH LATER, after returning to the fourteenth century, Kensa and Toran were wed amid the ruins of Tairseach. They could have wed in Toran's manor or even the chieftain's castle, but they felt it was the best place to wed, as it was Tairseach and its mystery that had brought them together.

Upon returning to Toran's time, Diana, Iain, and Caomhain had been delighted to learn of their engagement. Toran's sons had taken an instant liking to Kensa, thanking her for making their father happy.

Now, as the stiuireadh who performed their

ceremony announced that they were husband and wife, a happiness Toran had never felt before swept over him.

"My Kensa," he whispered, before their lips met in a kiss. "My enchantress. My wife. I love ye so."

~

DID YOU ENJOYED THIS NOVELLA? *Please consider leaving a review. Thank you!*

GLOSSARY

Below please find a glossary of magical terms used in this novella.

aingidh - a stiuireadh who uses magic for dark purposes

aosu tapa - the aging and de-aging process that affects some stiuireadh, giving them the appearance of seeming much older—or younger—than their actual age, all in the space of minutes

salachar - a term / slur for humans or those who do not possess magical abilities

stiuireadh - a witch or witches who possess the ability to travel through time

Tairseach - a time-travel portal located in the Scottish Highlands

Highlander Fate Series

Eadan's Vow

Ronan's Captive

Ciaran's Bond

Niall's Bride

Artair's Temptress

Latharn's Destiny

Highlander Fate Omnibus Books 1-3

Highlander Fate, Lairds of the Isles Series

Gawen's Claim

Bhaltair's Pledge

Domhnall's Honor

ABOUT THE AUTHOR

Stella Knight writes time travel romance and historical romance novels. She enjoys transporting readers to different times and places with vivid, nuanced heroes and heroines.

She resides in sunny southern California with her own swoon-worthy hero and her collection of too many books and board games. She's been writing for as long as she can remember, and when not writing, she can be found traveling to new locales, diving into a new book, or watching her favorite film or documentary. She loves romance, history, mystery, and adventure, all of which you'll find in her books.

Stay in touch!
stellaknightbooks.com